The Can-Do Thanksgiving

by Marion Hess Pomeranc

Pictures by Nancy Cote

Albert Whitman & Company

Morton Grove, Illinois

To my nephew, Sandy Hess, who's never a pea-brain. —M.H.P.

To Mike and the Coyle and Cassidy High School Food Pantry. —N.C.

Library of Congress Cataloging-in-Publication Data

Pomeranc, Marion Hess.

The can-do Thanksgiving / by Marion Hess Pomeranc: illustrated by Nancy Cote.

p. cm.

Summary: Dee experiences excitement and satisfaction when she helps
prepare and serve food for the needy at a church on Thanksgiving.

ISBN 0-8075-1054-8

[1. Thanksgiving Day—Fiction.] I. Cote, Nancy, ill. II. Title.   PZ7.P76955Can 1998   [E]—dc21   98-11264

CIP AC

The paintings were done in watercolor, pencil, and gouache.

The text typeface is Ulissa Rounded.

The design is by Scott Piehl.

Albert Whitman & Company is also the publisher of The Boxcar Children® Mysteries.

For more information about all our fine books, visit us at www.awhitmanco.com.

Dee searched Buster's Market for the just-right can.
"Corn?" suggested her mother. "Little-bitty white potatoes?"
"No," said Dee. She pushed her glasses higher on her nose.
"Peas!" she finally announced. "Please."

Dee proudly plunked her peas on the checkout counter. "They're for my class's Thanksgiving 'Can-Do' Food Drive," she told Priscilla, the cashier. "We bring cans and stuff to school, and later they get delivered to people who need them . . . somewhere."

Then Dee gave Priscilla the eighty-nine pennies which she'd saved by herself.

"Where will my peas go?" Dee asked her mother as they crossed the street to school.

"To a hungry person, for a nice meal," replied her mom.

Where? Dee wanted to ask, but it was time to go inside.

In her classroom, Dee placed her peas in a box at the front of the room. Hector plopped in a can of tuna. Keisha added fruit cocktail. Everybody brought something.

"It's almost time for the pick-up," Mrs. Ortiz, Dee's teacher, said.

Dee's can was about to disappear forever! She ran to her desk and grabbed a yellow sticker. DEE'S PEAS, OAK ST. SCHOOL, she wrote across it. Dee taped the note onto the can and whispered a secret wish: "I want to see where my peas go."

Hector heard her. He yelled, "No way, pea-brain!"

That evening, Dee and her father made their famous Veggie Medley. But Dee still had peas on her mind.

"Where did my can go?" she asked her father.

"Maybe to a food pantry or a soup kitchen," he said. "It'll be helpful . . . somewhere."

Hector was right! Dee would never know the fate of her peas.

But a week later, Mrs. Ortiz had a surprise.

"A church downtown received our 'Can-Do' cans—though it's a mystery how they knew where they came from . . ."

Dee looked at Hector and grinned.

Mrs. Ortiz continued. "Now they've invited us to help their volunteers serve and share a Thanksgiving meal at their soup kitchen. On Thursday at noon, I'll take anyone who'd like to go."

Hector gasped. Maybe Dee wasn't a pea-brain after all!

That Thursday, a boy named Tyler walked into the soup kitchen behind his mother. He felt a little shy because he'd never been there before. But his mom wanted him to have a real Thanksgiving meal. "Next year, we'll have Thanksgiving in a place of our own," she promised.

"I know," Tyler said, pushing his glasses higher on his nose. Just then a group of children rushed by. Tyler noticed a girl who wore glasses like his. *She might make a fun friend,* he thought.

Dee looked around. She saw tables being wiped. Floors being swept. People rushing in from the cold.

In the kitchen, Dee spotted crisp brown turkeys, a super-size kettle of soup, steaming stuffing, mashed potatoes, cranberry relish, and about a million green beans. There was someone stacking rolls, someone filling gravy boats, someone cutting pies into slices. But Dee didn't see a solitary pea.

"Welcome! We're so glad you're here,"
said a lady with a tray. "I need helpers for
serving." Keisha and Hector were her first volunteers.
"I need table setter-uppers!" called a man. Several
children shot to his side.
"And I need a napkin hander-outer," came a familiar
voice. It was Priscilla from Buster's Market! She was a
volunteer, too!

Dee walked through the dining room giving out napkins.

The tables were now crowded, and she saw a boy who wore glasses like hers.

The boy smiled at Dee. It made her think, *He'd be a fun friend, maybe…*

"Emergency!" The kitchen door blew open. Keisha
ran out, waving her hands. "Hector knocked over all the
vegetables!" she yelled. "Kablouey!"
  Dee raced back to help.

"The beans are history!" cried Priscilla as she plucked some from Hector's ear. "Dee, get me more vegetables, *fast!*" She pointed to the pantry.

Dee grabbed cans of carrots, beans, and zucchini. She brushed an entire row of canned corn into a basket.

Then, on the uppermost shelf, Dee saw a yellow sticker glimmering in the light. Her peas!

Dee stretched, hopped, then jumped. The peas were just too high. She was about to give up when . . .

. . . the boy with glasses offered Dee a chair.

"Hi, I'm Tyler," he said.

"Thanks, Tyler! I'm Dee." Dee climbed on and reached her peas.

Tyler tossed cans of tomatoes into the basket. Dee flung in more cans of peas.

"DEEEE! Hurry—everyone's waiting!" Priscilla called from the kitchen.

"TYLER! Where are you?" his mom called from the dining room.

"Yikes! Gotta go!" exclaimed Dee and Tyler at the same time. And they ran off in opposite directions.

Inside the kitchen, Priscilla looked worried. "What can we make with this mishmosh of cans?" she asked.

"A Veggie Medley," Dee explained. "My dad and I make it all the time."

Priscilla reached for an enormous pot.

Dee whispered something to Priscilla. It was one more secret wish.

"Definitely," said Priscilla, darting out the door. When she returned, Tyler was at her side, rolling up his sleeves. "Ready, set, cook!" he said.

Dee and Tyler took turns opening cans and pouring vegetables into the pot. When things got steamy, they took turns wiping fog from their glasses.

Soon only one can remained.

Dee poured her peas into the pot.

"Just right!" she said.

A few minutes later, Dee and Tyler emerged from the kitchen with a brimming vegetable platter held high between them. Everyone burst into applause.

"Hooray!" cheered Keisha.
"Marvelous," admired Mrs. Ortiz.
"Chowtime!" yelled Hector. "Dig in!"

"Please wait, my friends!"
The room grew quiet and still.
An elderly man rose. "Let's first give thanks for the blessings of this day," he said.

Some people bowed their heads, some closed their eyes, some took the hand of their neighbor.

Dee smiled at Tyler. He gave her a big thumbs-up.
They both pushed their glasses higher on their noses.
"*Now* can we dig in?" asked Hector.
And everybody did.